To my mom

He will put you in His angels' charge
to guard you wherever you go.
They will support you on their hands
lest you hurt your foot against a stone.
Psalms 91:11,12

Many thanks to and for the good angels
who made this book possible,
especially Brad and Jo,
Jim Sherbahn and Kate Moses,
the folks at Candlewick, and Bruce McMillan.

First U.S. paperback edition 1996

The Library of Congress has cataloged the hardcover edition as follows:
Cowen-Fletcher, Jane.
Baby angels / [written and illustrated by] Jane Cowen-Fletcher.
Summary: Baby begins her day surrounded by angels who
keep her out of trouble and make sure that her parents keep her
close by when she tries to wander off.
ISBN 1-56402-666-3 (hardcover)
[1. Babies—Fiction. 2. Angels—Fiction. 3. Stories in rhyme.]
I. Title
PZ8.3.C8344Bab   1996   [E]—dc20   95-19911
ISBN 0-7636-0203-5 (paperback)

2 4 6 8 10 9 7 5 3 1

Printed in Hong Kong

This book was typeset in Stempel Schneidler.
The pictures were done in pastels.

Candlewick Press
2067 Massachusetts Avenue
Cambridge, Massachusetts 02140

B·A·B·Y
ANGELS

Jane Cowen-Fletcher

CANDLEWICK PRESS
CAMBRIDGE, MASSACHUSETTS

Baby angels watch me wake,
follow every move
I make.

Baby angels see me climb,
stop my tumbles
every time.

Baby angels say, "Uh-oh,"
when I decide it's
time to go.

"Uh-oh!"

"Uh-oh!"

Outside, where I want to be—
baby angels,
follow me!

Angels guard me as I go,
then tell the ones
who need to know.

Baby angels join my play.
But most of all,
throughout each day . . .

Baby angels keep me near
those who love and
hold me dear.